DRAGON NIGHT

J. R. Krause

putnam

G. P. PUTNAM'S SONS

Georgie is afraid of the night.

It's too dark with the lights off.

Too quiet with everyone asleep.

And being alone makes everything worse.

Suddenly, Georgie's favorite book falls to the floor with a thump.

The pages flutter open, sparking and crackling.

A brilliant light fills the room, and a dragon steps out!

Georgie has never seen a real dragon before.

"Shhh! I'm running away," whispers the dragon.

"I'm afraid of the knight."

"I'm afraid of the night, too," says Georgie.

"Then let's run away together," says the dragon.

Georgie scales the dragon's bumpy back.
Together, they launch from the window.
The dragon spreads its great wings, and up
they soar, high into the dark night sky.

Far below, a carnival sparkles like pirate treasure.
Merry music floats up with joyful cries.
"There is no night down there," says Georgie.
"There is no knight," replies the dragon slowly,
"but there is a castle."
So they fly on.

Soon, an endless blanket of city lights shines below.

Horns honk and sirens wail on the busy streets.

"There is no night down there," says Georgie.

"There is no knight," replies the dragon carefully,

"but there is a king."

So they fly on.

Next, they soar over a bright, noisy baseball game.

The crowd roars like a magnificent waterfall.

"There is no night down there," says Georgie.

"But there he is!" replies the dragon.

"On a very peculiar horse!"

Georgie and the dragon fly on quietly.

"I think we are talking about two different things," says the dragon gently.

Georgie is thinking.

"But why is a big dragon like you afraid of the knight?" he asks.

"Because the knight *hates* me!" cries the dragon.
"He carries a heavy sword, and he always wants to fight."

Georgie doesn't know what to say.
He never thought of it that way before.

They sail silently down to a grassy field.

"You know," says the dragon, "the night is dark, but it's not always scary."

Georgie isn't so sure.

"Look," says the dragon. "Without the darkness of night, we wouldn't see the stars."

Georgie had never seen shooting stars before.

"Listen," says the dragon. "The night is quiet and peaceful."

Georgie hears crickets play a soothing song.

Before long, he curls up against the warm dragon and drifts off to sleep.

But night doesn't last forever.
As the sun rises, Georgie and
the dragon swoop back home.

Now the dragon is worried. "In the daylight, everyone can see me."

"You need to hide," says Georgie.

But there is no place big enough . . .

for the dragon . . .

to hide.

Now Georgie is worried.

"You belong in the book," he says.

"But I want to stay here with you!" cries the dragon.

A tear bubbles up and steams like hot tea.

The dragon quietly sniffs. "I'm still afraid of the knight."

"I have an idea," says Georgie.
"I'll make a new book for you
with a friendly knight."

"Will the knight carry a heavy
sword?" asks the dragon.
"Instead of a sword, the knight
will have a baseball and a glove,"
replies Georgie.

"Will the knight want to fight?" asks the dragon.

"Instead of fighting, the knight loves to play catch," replies Georgie.

"What if the knight doesn't like me?" asks the dragon.

"Don't worry," says Georgie. "I'll help you."

He turns the page . . .

. . . and draws a carnival with a carousel,
a candy shop filled with tasty treats,
a big, empty baseball field,
and the knight, waiting for a friend.

"The book is ready,"
says Georgie. "You'll
like this story."

"Thank you,"
replies the dragon.

A dazzling light fills the room once again as the dragon steps into the new book and gently waves goodbye.

KNiGHTS

Now every night, after a flight,
Georgie and the dragon snuggle up
and read their new favorite book.

"Good knight," says the dragon as
Georgie turns the last page.

"Good night," says Georgie.

Then, together in the dark and
quiet night, they fall fast asleep.

For Konrad,
in loving memory of his mom,
Kaitlin Kossakowski

G. P. PUTNAM'S SONS
an imprint of Penguin Random House LLC
375 Hudson Street
New York, NY 10014

Library of Congress Cataloging-in-Publication Data
Names: Krause, J. R., author, illustrator.
Title: Dragon night / J. R. Krause.
Description: New York, NY : G. P. Putnam's Sons, [2019]
Summary: Georgie is afraid of the dark, but after an adventure with a dragon that
is afraid of the knight in the book where he normally dwells, both are ready to sleep.
Identifiers: LCCN 2017019462 | ISBN 9780525514244 (hardcover) |
ISBN 9780525514251 (epub fixed) | ISBN 9780525514275 (kf8/kindle)
Subjects: | CYAC: Fear of the dark—Fiction. | Dragons—Fiction. | Bedtime—Fiction. | Books—Fiction.
Classification: LCC PZ7.1.K7338 Dr 2019 | DDC [E]—dc23
LC record available at https://lccn.loc.gov/2017019462

Manufactured in China by RR Donnelley Asia Printing Solutions Ltd.
ISBN 9780525514244
1 3 5 7 9 10 8 6 4 2

Design by Dave Kopka. Text in Kinesis Std.
The art was rendered with brush, pen, and ink on
cotton rag paper and then colored digitally.